Dear Parents:

Congratulations! Your child is taking the first steps on an exciting journey. The destination? Independent reading!

STEP INTO READING® will help your child get there. The program offers five steps to reading success. Each step includes fun stories and colorful art or photographs. In addition to original fiction and books with favorite characters, there are Step into Reading Non-Fiction Readers, Phonics Readers and Boxed Sets, Sticker Readers, and Comic Readers—a complete literacy program with something to interest every child.

Learning to Read, Step by Step!

Ready to Read   Preschool–Kindergarten
• big type and easy words • rhyme and rhythm • picture clues
For children who know the alphabet and are eager to begin reading.

Reading with Help   Preschool–Grade 1
• basic vocabulary • short sentences • simple stories
For children who recognize familiar words and sound out new words with help.

Reading on Your Own   Grades 1–3
• engaging characters • easy-to-follow plots • popular topics
For children who are ready to read on their own.

Reading Paragraphs   Grades 2–3
• challenging vocabulary • short paragraphs • exciting stories
For newly independent readers who read simple sentences with confidence.

Ready for Chapters   Grades 2–4
• chapters • longer paragraphs • full-color art
For children who want to take the plunge into chapter books but still like colorful pictures.

STEP INTO READING® is designed to give every child a successful reading experience. The grade levels are only guides; children will progress through the steps at their own speed, developing confidence in their reading.

Remember, a lifetime love of reading starts with a single step!

Thomas the Tank Engine & Friends ™ CREATED BY BRITT ALLCROFT

Based on the Railway Series by the Reverend W Awdry
© 2018 Gullane (Thomas) LLC. Thomas the Tank Engine & Friends and
Thomas & Friends are trademarks of Gullane (Thomas) LLC.
Thomas the Tank Engine & Friends and Design is Reg. U.S. Pat. & Tm. Off.
© 2018 HIT Entertainment Limited. HIT and the HIT Entertainment logo are
trademarks of HIT Entertainment Limited.
All rights reserved. Published in the United States by Random House Children's
Books, a division of Penguin Random House LLC, 1745 Broadway, New York,
NY 10019, and in Canada by Penguin Random House Canada Limited, Toronto.
Adapted from *The Runaway Kite*, first published in Great Britain by Egmont
UK Ltd., in 2012. *The Runaway Kite* copyright © 2012 Gullane (Thomas) LLC.

Step into Reading, Random House, and the Random House colophon are registered
trademarks of Penguin Random House LLC.

Visit us on the Web!
StepIntoReading.com
rhcbooks.com
www.thomasandfriends.com

ISBN 978-0-399-55768-2 (trade) — ISBN 978-1-5247-6903-1 (lib. bdg.)

Printed in the United States of America
10 9 8 7 6 5 4 3 2 1

Random House Children's Books supports the First Amendment
and celebrates the right to read.

HiT entertainment

THOMAS
& FRIENDS™

THE RUNAWAY KITE

Based on the Railway Series by the Reverend W Awdry

Random House 🏠 New York

It was a nice day.

The sky was blue.

Thomas picked up a box

at the Docks.
The box was for
the Kite Festival.

On the way,
Thomas saw a kite.

Oh, no!

The kite flew away!

Thomas wanted
to catch the kite.

Edward wanted to help.

But Thomas wanted
to catch the kite
by himself.
He went fast.

Emily wanted to help.

But Thomas wanted
to catch the kite
by himself.
He went faster.

Percy wanted to help.

But Thomas wanted
to catch the kite
by himself.
He went even faster!

Thomas found the kite!
But now Thomas was
out of steam.

He could not
catch the kite.
He could not
deliver the box.

Edward had steam!

Emily had steam!

Percy had steam!

The three friends
helped Thomas.
They caught the kite.

The kite flew
at the Kite Festival.

Thomas was happy
to have good friends.